PATH TO JUNGLETOWN

The Three Gray Stones

JUNGLETOWN

THE DEEPEST, DARKEST PART

For Claire, Tom and Maddy with a jungleful of love.

First published in the United States
by Phyllis Fogelman Books
An imprint of Penguin Putnam Books for Young Readers
345 Hudson Street
New York, New York 10014

Published in Great Britain
by Frances Lincoln Limited
Library of Congress Cataloging-in-Publication
Data available upon request
ISBN 0-8037-2671-6
Printed in Hong Kong

1 3 5 7 9 10 8 6 4 2

The illustrations were made using a combination of pencil,
ink, and watercolor. The images were then cut out
and pasted onto colored papers.

Visit the Anholts' website at www.anholt.co.uk

Chimp and Zee

 CATHERINE AND
LAURENCE ANHOLT

PHYLLIS FOGELMAN BOOKS NEW YORK

This is Chimp. This is Zee.

This is their home in a coconut tree.

Mumkey is hungry, but there are no bananas in the basket. "Which little monkeys have eaten all the bananas?" she says.

Up jumps Chimp.
Up jumps Zee.
"Ha, ha, ha!"
"Hee, hee, hee!"

So Chimp and Zee and Mumkey
go to Jungletown to buy more bananas.

Everyone is busy in Jungletown.

"It is easy to get lost,"
says Mumkey. "So stay close
and don't monkey around."
"Ha, ha, ha!" says Chimp.
"Hee, hee, hee!" says Zee.

Chimp and Zee
think shopping is boring.
They do NOT stay close to Mumkey.
They DO monkey around.

They look for a place to hide.
They find a small gray stone.

"Wherever are those naughty monkeys?" says Mumkey.

Up jumps Chimp.
Up jumps Zee.
"Ha, ha, ha!"
"Hee, hee, hee!"

Chimp and Zee find
a better place to hide —
behind a middle-sized gray stone.

"Wherever are those naughty
monkeys?" says Mumkey.

Up jumps Chimp.
Up jumps Zee.
"Ha, ha, ha!"
"Hee, hee, hee!"

Chimp and Zee find the best hiding place —
inside the banana basket
right on top of the
biggest gray stone of all.

"Ha, ha, ha!"
"Hee, hee, hee!"
"You can't find Chimp."
"You can't find Zee."

Then a remarkable thing happens.
The three gray stones begin to wobble . . .
The three gray stones begin to shake . . .
The three gray stones begin to rumble . . .
Then the three gray stones
get up and . . .

slowly walk away.

"Stop! Stop! STOP!" squeals Chimp.
"I want Mumkey!" squeals Zee.

Mumkey has finished shopping.

She is ready to go home.

"Wherever is my banana basket?" she says.

"Wherever are those three gray stones?" she says.

"But most of all — wherever are my little monkeys?" she cries.

And this time Chimp and Zee do NOT jump up at all.

Mumkey looks high.

Mumkey looks low.

Nobody has seen the banana basket.
Nobody has seen three gray stones.
Nobody has seen two little monkeys.

Everybody is going home.

"Perhaps they have gone back by themselves," says a policeman.

Mumkey goes home as fast as she can. But Chimp and Zee are NOT waiting in the coconut tree. "Deary, deary me! Wherever are Chimp and Zee?"

THIS is where they are — far, far away,
in the deepest, darkest part of Jungletown.
And still the three gray stones keep walking.

The night animals begin to growl — closer, closer, closer.

Chimp and Zee cuddle up together, underneath
the bananas at the very bottom of the banana basket.

Poor little Chimp.
Poor little Zee.
"Boo, hoo, hoo!"
"Wee, wee, weee!"

Then another remarkable thing happens.

The three gray stones are tired . . .

The three gray stones are thirsty . . .

The three gray stones go swimming . . .

The banana basket slips slowly into the river and . . .

gently floats away.

"Help! Help! HELP!" shouts Chimp.

"Wee! Wee! WEEE!" shouts Zee.

At home in the coconut tree, Mumkey looks sadly at the empty beds and the moonlit river outside.

Then the most remarkable thing of all happens.

Mumkey sees a basket . . .

The basket floats closer . . .

It is full of bananas . . .

The basket begins to wobble . . .

Up jumps Chimp.
Up jumps Zee.
"Ha, ha, ha!"
"Hee, hee, hee!"

Chimp and Zee kiss and cuddle and
chitter and chatter and monkey around and . . .
eat every single banana in the banana basket.

Good night, Chimp.
Good night, Zee.

Fast asleep in the coconut tree.